Signed Books and more

THE SUICIDE CLUB

Matt Shaw

This book is not making light of suicide.

In the last 45 years it is reported that suicide rates have increased by 60% worldwide.

Suicide is now among the three leading causes of death among those aged 15-44 (male and female).

If you find yourself struggling with suicidal thoughts then please do not suffer alone. You are not alone. Talk to someone, be it a friend of a doctor.

Talk to someone.

As one story ends, another begins.

The pale moonlight barely penetrated the thick blanket of fog. With all streetlights out, s*he* could barely see as she ran through the twisting maze of back-alleys. Every few steps she called for help but no one came. For the first time in her life, despite thinking she had felt it many times before, she knew what it meant to be truly alone. Another cry for help went unheard as the distant thunder rumbled overhead, closer than before. The storm was coming just as the weatherman had predicted. She knew it wasn't "just" a storm. She knew *what* was coming and only now was she starting to realise there was no running from it, just as she previously had been warned.

She turned down another narrow back-alley, tripping over an old, battered garbage can in the process; the contents of which spilled out before her. She climbed to her feet and continued running only to turn into a dead-end. Panic. She turned in perfect time with another clap of thunder from directly above now, which was promptly followed by a crackle of lightning. The clap rumbled on at a low pitch, shaking her insides. The tiny hairs on the back of her neck and arms stood, thanks to the static in the air.

She screamed, 'Leave me alone.'

There was a voice. Deep. Quiet. Smooth. Haunting. 'Why are you running? This is what you wanted, isn't it? Why run from what you want?' The voice came from no direction in particular, just bouncing around inside her head with a faint echo.

She screamed again. 'Leave me alone!'

With nowhere else to go, she backed up against the brick wall of the dead-end. Tears ran freely down her pale face, a couple of which she wiped away with the back of her shaking hand. Her voice was quieter the next time she begged, 'Leave me alone!'

The other voice, circling around in her terrified mind, simply replied, 'I can't.'

She dropped to her knees as, all around her, the many dark shadows started to stretch out towards her.

1

Greg Dolman woke with a start, which also startled his mother and father who were sitting at his bedside with concerned looks upon their faces. His eyes were slow to focus due to the medication flowing through his system but, when they did, he realised he was lying, tucked up, in a hospital bed. His mouth was dry. His head ached. Various noisy machines were lined up by his side, beeping and whirring. He felt his mother squeeze his hand and - still dazed - he glanced in her direction. She was talking yet he heard no words, only a piercing ringing. Slowly - with the more she spoke - her words started to mean something to him other than "noise".

'Are you okay? How are you feeling?'

The look on her face made him feel sick with guilt. At least that was what he presumed it to be. It could have been the meds causing the nauseous feeling bubbling in his tummy. Still, unable to look at his worried parents, he turned away from them.

'Greg?'

Greg was sitting in a doctor's surgery. A doctor was looking directly at him from behind his overly large desk on which was scattered various files and scribbled notes. Greg was staring out of the window at his side. Outside the world looked so quiet and peaceful from this window. The view itself was nothing more than a large, green meadow. In the distance there was the edge of a woodland area. It looked serene despite the fact Greg knew there was a loud motorway on the other side of the small woodland and, had the office been on the other side of the building, he could have been staring at a noisy builders' yard.

The doctor said his name again, 'Greg?'

Greg snapped back to the room and turned his dwindling attention back to the doctor. The doctor was an older man. Bald yet with a bushy grey beard, thick rimmed glasses and one tooth more yellow than the others which Greg never could get his head around.

The doctor asked, 'Have you been taking your medication?'

Greg nodded.

'And how are you feeling?'

Greg was on his knees in his bathroom. On the tiled floor next to him was an empty pill bottle. The pills themselves were scattered all around. Tears streamed down Greg's face as the old memory of his mother and father flashed back to mind. Their faces staring at him when he had woken up in the hospital.

'I feel fine,' Greg said. He looked the doctor dead in the eye when he said it. To anyone else, they would have believed him, but the doctor had seen this lie from many different people in a number of different circumstances over the years. He knew Greg had his walls up and, furthermore, he understood why. On the one hand it was easier to say everything was okay then admit to struggling and - on the other hand - Greg had been close to getting sectioned after his last suicide attempt; something he was desperate to avoid for obvious reasons. Despite the lie, the doctor knew not to press too hard. Past experience had long since taught him that the harder you push, the more a person runs. Besides, he only had ten minutes per patient and pushing could have opened a can of worms he didn't have time for.

'I think we should meet again in a couple of weeks,' the doctor said. His words winded Greg. Greg had hoped that this would be it now. He'd agreed to the medication, he had agreed to these regular appointments to "check-in", he had done *everything* they had asked and in doing so, he'd hoped they'd at least cut back on these sessions. Greg perceived them as a waste of time, not just for him but for the doctor too. There could have been someone else out there who was more in need of the appointment slot, someone who'd not already made their mind up about how their life was to play out.

The doctor printed out a prescription. It was for another month's worth of tablets. He held the slip out to Greg who just looked at it. 'You're running low so this will keep you going.'

Greg just bit his tongue and sighed. He found it amusing how he had tried to take his own life with a bunch of sleeping tablets and - straight out of hospital - he had been issued yet more pills. They said it was to try and help with his moods but so far, he'd felt nothing except increased agitation and - because of that - he started to wonder whether they'd actually given him the pills so he could have another go at topping himself. Funnier yet, to him, was how "increased suicidal thoughts" was listed as a side effect. Did they really want to help? They pretended as much, hence the fortnightly appointments to see how he was getting on with everything.

Greg leaned forward to take the slip. As he did so, the black sleeve of his shirt rolled up a fraction revealing beneath a fresh tattoo inked to his skin. The doctor noticed and as Greg took the prescription from him, he asked, 'New ink?'

Greg nodded. 'Yeah.'

'Nice. Can I see it? I've always wanted a tattoo but might put off some of the older patients I see. They'll probably think I'm a thug.' He laughed. The doctor didn't care about tattoos and had never wanted one but he knew it was a quick bit of conversation he could have, before they parted ways, in which he could appear as more than "just" a doctor.

Greg pulled his sleeve back and showed him the artwork: a greyscale portrait of a Death's-Head moth.

'Well, isn't that something,' the doctor said. Tattoos weren't to his taste but, with this one at least, there was no denying the beautiful line work and shading. 'Looks sore,' he said with a laugh.

Greg pulled his sleeve back into position and said, 'It's fine.' He stood up and pocketed the prescription in his jacket. He already knew he wouldn't be taking it to the pharmacy to swap it over for the meds. His life had taken a different turn since he'd last seen the doctor and this new direction needed no prescriptions, only time.

One year to be exact.

2

Greg was just sitting in his car, parked up in the doctor's carpark. He never just drove off after an appointment because his temper was always higher than before he'd gone in. He found the doctors to be a waste of time; they pretended to care by talking the talk but - really - he knew he was just a number to them. He also knew that he stopped mattering to them the moment he left the office. To sit there, on these forced appointments, with someone who had better things to be doing was just frustrating. It was even more frustrating when it was a different doctor too. Another face to see because the other person was "busy" or had a day off. The "new" doctor would always ask Greg to wait a moment whilst he scanned through the notes and - then - it would be the same dance as all the other sessions.

Are you taking your medications?

How are you feeling?

Anything on your mind?

Any more suicidal thoughts?

Do you have enough tablets left or need some more?

Want to try a stronger dosage?

To Greg, it was nothing more than waste of his time. Time. Slightly less than a year now and then none of this would matter. No more appointments, no more guilt as to what he'd put his family through, no more tablets, no more dark thoughts, struggles. There'd only be what had been promised to him - and that was "nothing". He smiled at such a blissful thought. He just wished he could sleep the remaining time away. Like a kid at Christmas wishing December away, he wished he could just close his eyes and wake up on *the* day. The support group he was a part of - others signed up to this scheme - had their own plans for their last year but, fuck that. He didn't want to "go out with a bang", or "make the most of the time to tell people how I really felt about them" or whatever stupid suggestions had been spoken about at the last group meeting. He just wanted it over with. Truth be told he didn't even understand why they needed this last year. That was the scheme's rules, not the patrons' choice. Still, he'd play their game if it meant things would be easier when the time came and, in the great scheme of things, a year wasn't that long.

Greg's mobile phone started to ring from his inside pocket. He laughed to himself and shook his head. Like clockwork, every time he had an appointment with the doctor. He didn't need to look at the screen to see who it was. Oh, to be able to ignore it. No chance of that though for he knew she would just keep calling and calling and calling until he answered. He asked her why, once, but she just said she was being supportive. Funny. Had she been supportive back when they were dating, he might not have made that first attempt. Anyway, she had met someone else, why did she care anymore? Especially as it had been her choice to leave him in the first place! Had she cared, like she pretended, she wouldn't have left. She would have worked through their problems and carried on trying to make a go of things but, no, she just packed her shit and got the hell out of there. He pushed the painful memories from mind and reached for his phone. Sure enough, her name was on the screen.

Greg answered the phone, 'I'm fine.'

That was all she really wanted; to know how he was. She knew the appointments with the doctor riled him up so she'd always make a point of calling in a hope that hearing her voice, and words of encouragement, would help to calm him own. He didn't tell her as such but, half the time it actually hurt more to hear her voice. Her choice to leave.

Her choice. Had it been down to Greg, they'd still be together.

'How was the appointment?'

'Yeah. Great. They've cured me,' Greg said sarcastically. In response, his ex-partner Nikki Fontana sighed down the phone. Greg didn't apologise for his sarcasm, but he did ask, 'I'm not sure what you want me to say?'

'What I've always wanted from you; the truth.'

'You realise these people are just ticking boxes, right? I did what I did, it didn't go to plan, to show society gives a shit they force you into these appointments under the guise of "helping". They don't care. They never will and I don't know why you can't get that in your head.'

'I know it might not feel like…'

Greg cut her off, 'Trust me - they don't give a shit. I know you want me to be okay and to stop this dark cloud forming above my head but, that's who I am and who I have been for as long as I can remember and…'

Nikki cut him off, 'You weren't like that when we first got together.'

Greg laughed. 'Or I just hid it well.' The moment the words escaped his lips he regretted them. 'As I keep saying, I don't know why you call.'

'And as I keep saying; because I care.'

There was a pause. Greg asked, 'How's James?'

Nikki sighed audibly. She had been dating James Steel for a few months now. Not that Greg believed her when she told him so but, James hadn't been the reason Greg and Nikki had broken up. They broke up because Greg was too closed off. Nikki could see him shutting down further and further each day and nothing she said, or did, seemed to snap him out of it. If she hadn't got out of the relationship then, Greg would have dragged her down with him and she couldn't allow that. To answer his question, she answered, 'James is fine.'

'Well good for James. I'm happy for him. And you.'

Nikki changed the subject, 'Are you taking your pills still?'

Greg laughed. 'Everyone is so interested in me taking these fucking pills. I should start an *Only Fans* page, shouldn't I? Video myself necking these tablets and charge people a subscription to watch.'

'We just want to know…'

'… That you're not going to have to clean up my corpse…'

'No that's….'

'Well, you don't have to worry about that…'

'I didn't mean…'

'… and you haven't had to worry about that for a while now. We aren't a couple. You only ever call me when I've had an appointment at the doctors. You don't call any other time… I don't know what you want but seriously - just stop. You left me and you moved on with some other prick. Good for you. Hearing your voice just rubs that in and…' He didn't know why he was explaining himself when he could just hang up on her which is exactly what he did.

Despite the way the conversation had ended, there was no bitterness on Greg's part. He wasn't angry. He wasn't even annoyed that she'd called. Any of those feelings would have meant he would have had to feel something, and Greg hadn't felt any real emotion for a long, long time now. Greg tossed the phone to the passenger seat of his car and fired up the car's cold engine. Just as Nikki always called him up after an appointment, regular as clockwork, he too had a routine of his own after such a session and, for Greg, it started at the local bar. As he pulled out of the doctor's surgery, a question popped into his mind: *Would Yolanda Lamas be there*? If she was, he knew the company he'd signed with was nothing more than a crock of shit conning the guilty out of money. If she wasn't then... Greg paused in thought for a moment. He wasn't sure how he should feel if she wasn't there...

The bar was in a busy part of town but, despite the hustle and bustle in the surrounding streets, the pub always seemed quiet. It was popular with the locals, who were always accommodating to visitors, and nicely decked out with a pool table and juke box which was mostly filled with Pink Floyd records. Outside the pub, a street away, there was a large underground car park which was perfect for those who wanted to drive in and get a taxi home safe in the knowledge their vehicle would be safe for a night. Of course, most people who wanted to go to the drinking establishment to drink got a cab both ways but it was nice to have the option. Besides - sometimes people had no intention of going into the bar and just happened to find themselves there after a busy, stressful day or because a friend dragged them there. A friend like Yolanda Lamas.

3.

Greg walked into the bar and looked around at all the faces in there. Most of them he recognised, not that he knew their names. Some of them looked up to see who'd walked in but most stayed wrapped up in their own conversation or staring down to the bottom of their drink. A couple smiled at Greg as they recognised him but, he didn't respond back to them. Instead, he walked over to the bar and sat on one of the old, tatty stools.

The bartender walked over, 'The usual?'

'Sure.' As the bartender started pouring Greg his usual post-surgery pint, Greg asked, 'You seen Yolanda today?'

The bartender glanced up from his pint-pouring with a confused look on his face. He asked, 'Who?'

'Yolanda? You know. Dark hair... Pretty... Fucked her way through most of the bar.'

The bartender laughed. 'Ha! I think I'd recognise someone like that. She sounds like fun though for sure so, if you find her, by all means bring her in for a drink.' He finished pouring the pint from the tap and set the glass down in front of Greg who was just sitting there with a confused look on his face. The bartender knew Yolanda. Going by what she'd told Greg, they'd even fucked before now - out the back amongst the trash cans, class woman that she is - so Greg had no idea why he was pretending not to know her. Also, it had been Yolanda who'd introduced Greg to this place after they'd had one of the weekly meetings in the old hall around the corner from here.

'Hey, John, get us another one, will you?' a man called out from across the bar. John, the bartender, gave the other fella a nod and headed over to fetch his drink, leaving Greg in his state of confusion.

Greg shook his confusion away and took his phone from out of his jacket pocket. The bartender was clearly just being a prick today, for whatever reason. Maybe he was jealous of how close Greg and Yolanda seemed to be? After all - since meeting - they'd been in the bar drinking together most days and often left together. *Making the most of her time left*, Yolanda had called it. Her excuse to act like a slut and fuck anyone and everyone without even caring if they wore protection or not. *What does it matter? I'm dead anyway.* Her words rung through Greg's mind as clear as they had sounded when she first explained her habits to him. He laughed at the time. *One year left and you want to risk getting pregnant?* He wore a condom.

'The fuck?' he muttered to himself as he scrolled through his text messages to find their most recent one. It hadn't been long since they'd last spoken via text and yet - weirdly - her messages were gone. He closed the app down and went to contacts; with no recent message he'd have to go the long way round to her number. A few scrolls later though and he frowned. Her number was missing from his phone entirely. 'This is ridiculous…' Confused, he searched a couple of other random names which popped to mind; a test to see if more numbers were missing. They weren't. Only Yolanda's had gone. 'Shit.' He set his phone down and looked towards the door in the hope that it would open at any minute and she would walk in, with her usual "forced smile". The problem was, deep down he knew she wouldn't be coming back. Not today and not ever.

As the realisation sunk in, he turned away from the door and stared down into his pint. Yolanda had been doing it the right way; drinking every day and spending the last year of her life with a drunken haze around everyone and everything. In such a state, the world never seemed as bad. Although that only worked out in your favour when you had a definite ending in sight. Greg had watched his own father die of alcoholism and he knew it wasn't a pleasant way to go. That being said (or thought, at least) he sunk his pint in one and ordered another.

Fuck this day.

Fuck all the days.

4.

Part of the scheme Greg had signed up to meant he had to not only live one final year of life but also attend weekly group meetings with others who had signed up. As weird as it sounded, Greg didn't mind these meetings because everyone there knew why the other person was there. They didn't ask how they were doing; they didn't ask if they were still taking their medication, they didn't do anything but laugh at the rest of the world and talk about their plans for how they wanted to spend the last year. It was as though the knowledge of their own demise lifted the depression they'd been in. He guessed it was because there was a full stop awaiting them, which was known, as opposed to the possibility of living miserable for many more years to come with no end in sight. With that "full stop" being so close, nothing really seemed to be that bad anymore - especially with the additional knowledge in that, by doing it this way, their families and friends would be helped - *when the time came*. Of course, it helped that there were tea and biscuits. Who didn't love tea and biscuits?

It was 7pm on Friday. The meeting was due to start at half seven but, still curious about Yolanda, Greg had got there earlier to ask if anyone knew what had become of her. It had been four days since his doctor's appointment. Four days since he last heard from Nikki and four days of constant trips back to the same bar on the off-chance she would suddenly show up in there. Four days of just *wondering*. There was even a small part of him which wondered whether he should phone around the local hospitals to see if someone matching her description had shown up but - even if he had called, he doubted they would have told him. The not knowing was causing him stress with a small, selfish part of him hoping that she was okay even though he knew she would have been happier "dead".

Greg walked into the hall. He'd spent the afternoon in the bar around the corner and was a little unsteady on his feet, but he knew no one would give a shit. So long as guests weren't abusive to one another, no one cared about the state they arrived in. It was, after all, their final year so they were just living life how they wanted to. One guest, for example, had even turned to using smack. He'd always been curious about drugs; wondering what could be so great about them to cause people to throw their lives away chasing them. At the same time, he'd always been petrified of actually trying them too because he didn't want to become an addict and ruin his own life. Again, with the end in sight, it didn't matter if he became an addict for the last few months. It made sense in his head.

As Greg took his seat amongst those who'd also arrived early, he didn't waste time in asking, 'Anyone heard from Yolanda?' All of them looked at him like he was speaking some kind of foreign language. When no one answered him immediately, he asked, 'Anyone? Anyone heard from Yolanda?'

Robyn Mattern was the first to ask, 'Who?'

'For fuck sake not you lot as well.' Greg rolled his eyes and explained, 'Come on, I just want to know that everything went as she'd hoped it would.'

Robyn asked again, 'Who are you talking about?'

'Yolanda Lamas! Yolanda! Come on, she's been coming here for a fucking year. We've all been to the pub together... Robyn, I've even watched you talking to her on multiple occasions so - come on - did everything go okay for her?'

Robyn shook her head and said, 'I honestly have no idea who you are talking about.'

'This is fucking stupid. I thought the whole point of this group was we were in this thing together. Just tell me!'

'I can't tell you what I don't know!' Robyn snapped back. The others, sitting with her, were visibly starting to get uncomfortable with the conversation when - from behind Greg - the hall door opened, and Chris Hall walked in.

As Chris walked towards the group, he called out, 'So what is everyone shouting about then? Can hear you from down the corridor.' His eyes fixed on Greg who - from his body language - was visibly agitated. 'All good, Greg?'

'Not really, no.'

'What seems to be the problem?'

Greg took a moment to compose himself. When he felt like he could talk without raising his voice, he said, 'I just want to know how it went with Yolanda.' Greg felt his face flush hot when Chris's expression changed to one of confusion. Was this prick really going to pretend she didn't exist as well? He went to say something before Chris cut in.

'We have a bit of time before the session starts, we should have a chat.' Chris didn't wait for Greg to agree. He just turned and walked back out of the room. Greg got up from his chair and shook his head towards the others.

He said, 'I don't know what the fuck is wrong with not just telling me how it went for her? Remind me not to give a shit when the same comes of any of you.' He walked off, following in the direction Chris had gone.

The hall was rented out for Friday sessions only. As a result, there wasn't an office Chris could have used with Greg so the pair of them were left standing in the corridor, away from the others.

Chris Hall was a typical suit. His black hair was slicked back, he wore what looked like a designer suit although hadn't bothered with a tie. His face was freshly shaven and he had the eyes of a shark. He waited for Greg to say something first, before he potentially said something he didn't actually need to.

'Yolanda Lamas,' Greg said. Before Chris could say anything, Greg added, 'And I swear to God, if you ask me who then - I'm going to swing for you.'

'Yolanda Lamas?'

'Jesus Christ, yes! Yolanda Lamas! She's been coming here for a year. A fucking year! Her time came to an end the other day and I've been asking around how it went for her, if it even did but everyone is pretending like they've never heard of her.' Greg stopped talking, almost exhausted.

There as a slight pause before Chris asked, 'Finished?'

'We were friends. I just want to know if...'

Chris cut him off and told him, 'People don't really make friends in this group. Short-lived thing and all that. They make acquaintances but not friends...'

'Even acquaintances wouldn't just forget someone.'

'No. No they wouldn't.'

'Yet they're all pretending like they never knew her. It's that easy to cut people out of their lives, is it?'

'They didn't forget her.'

'And yet that's *exactly* what they are pretending.'

'She never existed.'

'What?'

'Obviously, we need to talk about this but now isn't the time. I have a session to run and I can't stop that just to have a conversation with you. Now I am happy to talk to you, but we need to wait until after the session. Okay?'

Greg nodded reluctantly.

'Okay,' Chris continued. 'Good. Let's get back in there and get the session started, yes?' He didn't wait for Greg to respond or argue with him. Confused as to   how Greg seemed to know about Yolanda, Chris headed back into the room. Greg hesitated a moment and then followed, both confused and angry. The only reason he was trying harder to keep his cool was because he wanted answers. More specifically, he was started to wonder what he had signed up for.

5.

BEFORE

'You're not going to ask how I am?' Yolanda looked at Chris. He was standing opposite her in a small, empty office.

'I know how you are. It's why you're here.'

Yolanda didn't say anything. She was impressed he hadn't tried to fill in the uncomfortable silence with such a question, especially as it seemed everyone else in her life had when they'd visited her.

They stood for a few more minutes in silence when Chris finally asked her, 'Did you have any questions?'

'Do I have to keep this to myself? Like, can I tell people I've signed up? I mean, I'm not sure who I would tell but…'

Chris laughed. 'This isn't *Fight Club*. We have no rules. The only thing we ask is that you take a night to think about it because once you sign up, there's no refunds. Then when you sign up, we have a weekly meeting with other people who are a part of the program and we insist you come to those.'

'Why?'

'It's just something we do. We've found it helps people, such as you, to talk about the things they're going to do with their remaining time. It inspires others to follow suit, so no one is left wasting their time.'

'Ten thousand?'

'Ten thousand. A cheap price, don't you think?'

Yolanda laughed. This man was offering her a deal in which she paid him money, and, after a year, he helped with her suicide. Given she could have just gone out of the office, that very moment, and thrown herself in front of a train for free - ten grand didn't seem to be that brilliant a deal. But then she remembered, she wasn't paying the money to just end her life. The full deal was that they would help with that side of things but also ensure her family and friends were okay too. To them, she would be dead but not because she had taken her own life. She would just have been killed in a tragic accident and whilst they would grieve - they wouldn't be stuck with the horrible thought of how they could have saved her, if only they had paid her more attention. If only they had seen the signs. Ten grand to take that pain away from them. It *was* a cheap price to anyone with a conscience.

'You know why I am here.'

'Yes.'

'So why do I have to wait a year? Why can't we just get it done now?'

Chris nodded. He was expecting that question. It was the one *everyone* asked. 'Because people are often stuck in a black hole - with depression - because there is no end in sight. For those who know when they're going to die though, I mean the exact day and exact time, then they find themselves worrying less about day to day things which could have been keeping them bogged down in the darkness. They live more. They take that last year and fully embrace it and...'

'... And find a new zest for life and cancel the agreement?'

'Non-refundable,' Chris added with a smile.

'The small print.'

'Of course.' Chris continued, 'But you know, sometimes they don't do anything with that year. They wallow in self-pity and count down the days but, the majority of souls... Yeah... They start to appreciate things more.' Chris's final point was, 'And we also need a year to plan things out properly. We don't want to rush into things and make mistakes, do we?'

'Those weekly meetings; are we supposed to sit around and talk about God?'

'I don't know about you but, I don't believe in God.'

'Me neither.'

'Probably a waste of time having us sit around talking about him then, yes?'

'Yes.' Chris said, 'Like I said, you just talk about what you're doing and what you're looking forward to. The only thing we ask is that you don't just keep saying you're looking forward to your final day. We try and keep the meetings a bit more upbeat. As I said, we all know why you're there so there is no point dwelling on that. We want to see people make the most of their final year.' He paused a moment before he asked, 'What would you do with your last year on Earth?'

Yolanda laughed. 'Can I get drunk every day?'

Chris shrugged. 'If that's your idea of fun.'

'And I want to be a slut. Fuck anyone and everyone. I missed that part of my life when I was growing up. Too busy chasing the dreams that never came, to party with my friends so - yeah - I want to fuck.'

'See,' Chris said with a laugh, 'already sounds like fun!'

'Well, I don't think I need a night to think about it,' Yolanda said. 'Where do I sign up?'

'The contract is just between you and me. A verbal agreement, but to show you're into it, you have to have a tattoo with the date on it.'

'A verbal agreement? How do I know you won't just take the money and run?'

'We don't take payment until your last day.'

'Then how do you know I won't back out of paying if I change my mind and want to live with this newfound love of life?'

Chris smiled. 'No one has backed out yet.'

'What's the tattoo?'

'Death's-Head Moth and the first day of our agreement.'

'It doesn't have to go on my forehead, does it?'

Chris laughed. 'You can choose where it goes.'

'My arse cheek.'

'If that's what you want. I'm sure the tattooist won't care where it goes.'

'So, I get a tattoo, go to the weekly meetings and then a year later you help me to die. Then you make it so my family are as okay as they can be.'

'That's right. And, honestly, you won't regret having a year. You'll find your whole outlook changes.'

'But you said no one has backed out yet.'

'They haven't. But they've loved near enough every day of their last year.'

'I still don't know what is stopping me from going out and killing myself now.'

'The same thing that stopped you seeing it through properly the first time.'

Yolanda fell silent as she gazed down at the scar on her wrist. One wrist was scarred, one was fine. She'd made the first cut and then immediately called for help, unable to go through with it as thoughts of her family and friends finding her there flashed to mind.

Chris continued, 'If you need an evening to think about it.'

'No. Where do I get the tattoo? I mean, are they open 24 hours? Do I have to book in for an appointment which in itself could be a wait of a few months?'

Chris told her, 'No. We have someone who does the tattooing. As soon as you're ready we can make the call and get it booked in. It's usually same day. Not like it's a big tattoo.'

'Well,' Yolanda said, 'I don't need to think about this. My mind is made up.'

Chris smiled. 'Okay. So long as you're sure.' He concluded, 'I'll call the tattooist then.'

A YEAR LATER

The pale moonlight barely penetrated the thick blanket of fog. With all streetlights out, s*he* could barely see as she ran through the twisting maze of back-alleys. Every few steps she called for help but no one came. For the first time in her life, despite thinking she had felt it many times before, she knew what it meant to be truly alone. Another cry for help went unheard as the distant thunder rumbled overhead, closer than before. The storm was coming just as the weatherman had predicted. She knew it wasn't "just" a storm. She knew *what* was coming and only now was she starting to realise that there was no running from it, just as she'd been previously warned.

She turned down another narrow back-alley, tripping over an old, battered garbage can in the process; the contents of which spilled out before her. She climbed to her feet and continued running only to turn into a dead-end. Panic. She turned in perfect time with another clap of thunder from directly above now, which was promptly followed by a crackle of lightning. The clap rumbled on at a low pitch, shaking her insides. The tiny hairs on the back of her neck and arms stood, thanks to the static in the air.

She screamed, 'Leave me alone.'

There was a voice. Deep. Quiet. Smooth. Haunting. 'Why are you running? This is what you wanted, isn't it? Why run from what you want?' The voice came from no direction in particular and just bounced around inside her head with a faint echo.

She screamed again. 'Leave me alone!'

With nowhere else to go, she backed up against the brick wall of the dead-end. Tears ran freely down her pale face, a couple of which she wiped away with the back of her shaking hand. Her voice was quieter the next time she begged, 'Leave me alone!'

The other voice, bouncing around in her terrified mind, simply replied, 'I can't.'

She dropped to her knees as, all around her, the many dark shadows started to stretch out towards her.

6.

Greg said nothing during the meeting with the rest of those who'd signed up. He just sat there and listened, wondering if anyone else would bring up Yolanda. Unsurprisingly no one said anything about her and - as a result - Chris's words continued going over and over in his mind: *She had never existed.*

At the end of the meeting, Greg didn't move from his uncomfortable plastic seat. He just sat there with his eyes fixed directly on Chris who was saying goodbye to the others, individually, as they left.

Robyn came over to him with an unpleasant look on her face. She said to Chris, 'We're all meant to be in this together, making the most of the time left. Maybe it's best if you just stay away if you're going to come here with that negative attitude.'

Chris couldn't believe this. He had asked how his friend - and their colleague - was and suddenly he was the bad guy? He looked Robyn up and down and, instead of arguing with her, he just smiled. Then, he laughed.

'What's so funny?'

'I was just thinking,' Chris explained, 'that I hope it hurts.'

'What does?'

'Whichever means you die by, when your time comes.'

'What?!'

Chris explained again, 'When your time comes to die, I hope it is fucking painful, you nasty little bitch.'

Robyn stood there with a shocked look on her face. Her mouth was slightly ajar as though she were about to say something but there were no words to come out.

Chris continued, 'Did you tell your family or friends about this place? What you had signed up to?'

Robyn stuttered, 'Why would I?'

'I'm just curious as to how they would have reacted. Sad to your face, maybe. But then the moment you turned your back and walked away, I could just envision them throwing a massive party. Ding dong the witch is dead.'

'Fuck you,' Robyn hissed. She turned and walked towards the exit where Chris was saying goodbye to another person. He turned to her and smiled broadly, unaware of the conversation she'd just had with Greg. 'If he is still here next week, I won't be coming back.' She didn't wait for

Chris to say anything, she just barged past him and out of the door.

When it was just the two of them left in the hall, Chris closed the door and walked back over to the circle of seats. He sat opposite Greg. Greg didn't bother to say anything as he figured Chris already knew what he was waiting for.

Ignoring whatever the hell had been wrong with Robyn, Chris said, 'That was a good meeting. It's weird, isn't it, that these people all come in here with the sole aim of ending their lives and yet, as the meetings go on, they seem to be more and more cheerful. You know why? Because there is an end in sight. They're making the most of their time as opposed to dwelling on the *desire* to die, they already know they will die so… They start to think about living.' This was more or less the same crap Chris had spouted when Greg had first met him, soon after he'd been released from hospital after his second suicide attempt. Greg had thought it was bullshit then and, despite the rest of the group seeming to be happier, he still thought it was bullshit now. Even if he didn't, this wasn't what he wanted to discuss anyway.

To save on more inane conversation, Greg asked, 'What do you mean Yolanda never existed.'

'See, I know she existed because I'm the one who is running this. I remember everyone who had that tattoo inked to their skin,' he said as he looked towards the Death's-Head moth on Greg's wrist. 'I know them all. I remember their names. I remember their appearances. Even remember the sound of their voices and yet - weirdly - I don't remember what my own deceased mother and father sound like anymore. Weird that; I can remember the strangers easily but my own family members… Nothing.'

'I know she existed because I was having drinks with her most days and…' Greg stopped himself from saying anything else. Chris didn't need to know how they'd fuck from time to time or anything else that they got up to. It was none of his business. 'So, don't tell me she didn't exist because I met her, I hung out with her, I *knew* her. So, what happened to her?'

'What if I was to say that - at the end of your year - you'll cease to exist too?'

'I know. That's why I signed up.'

'No. You signed up to die. You signed up so we help you with that and help your family and friends afterwards.'

'Same thing.'

'Not at all. For you the result is the same and the one you wanted; you won't be here anymore. You'll be gone. You will cease to exist. But - in that - you will also cease to exist to everyone else too. They won't know you anymore. They'd never have heard of you... Your parents won't even know they'd ever had a child. You will simply be erased from history.'

'The fuck are you talking about?'

'No more pain for you, just as you wanted. No more pain for your loved ones either. Nothing. A perfect way to deal with this whole unpleasant business for those who wish to take their own life. Again, you get what you want and the people you leave behind live on without any knowledge or memories of you, or what you have done.'

'The fuck are you even talking about?' Greg could feel his temper start to rise but did his best to suppress it as he knew, if he lashed out, he'd get no more answers. Not that the answers he was getting made much sense to him. 'Then why didn't you explain it like that when we signed up?'

'Because then you wouldn't have signed up. You would have thought I were a mad man, just as you're probably thinking that now. The only difference is now you've seen it for yourself.'

'I've seen nothing. You say she doesn't exist, and that people won't remember her anymore and yet, I remember her.'

'And that is a big puzzle, right there. I've been doing this for more years than you'd realise or believe and I have never seen another person recall someone who'd been erased from history.'

'You're full of shit.'

'And yet everyone you talk to has no recollection of her...'

'You're all in this together. A big con to get ten grand out of me.'

Chris laughed. 'If that were the case, given the amount of people involved, we would probably be asking for more than ten grand, wouldn't we?'

Greg didn't have an answer for that. It wasn't a lot of money for such a complex scheme but, at the same time, none of what Chris was saying made sense. It wasn't possible to just have someone written out of the history books. God knows historians have tried it over the decades with a number of "darker" characters from the past. *People don't just get written out of history.*

There was a pause before Greg asked, 'So at the end of my time, I'm just going to "poof" into a cloud of smoke and - just like that - no one will remember me?'

'Well, I'll remember you but, yes, everyone else will forget you ever existed. There'll be no trace of you as everything goes.'

Greg realised he wasn't going to get anywhere talking to this prick. He just shook his head and stormed from the room. Chris said nothing to stop him. Even if Greg ran off telling people all about this, no one would believe him. With any luck, tomorrow, Greg would wake up in his bed and just shrug it all off. What will be, will be. At the end of his year, he is getting what he wanted anyway. The fact the other people would have zero pain to deal with, surely, he would be happy with that by the time he had processed everything because - really, in the great scheme of things - what had changed?

Chris shrugged. He got up and started to move the chairs to the corner of the room just as the owners of the hall had asked of him.

7.

Greg hadn't driven home. He was parked up outside Yolanda's home, unable to believe a damn word Chris Hall had told him. The only thing he kept thinking in his mind was that it was impossible to just delete someone from history. And - if it were possible - then her stuff wouldn't be in the house still.

Greg climbed from his car and crossed the road. Without any hesitation he stormed straight up the path and to her front door. He knocked loudly and waited.

From behind the door, he could hear the sound of movement as someone approached. It could have been Yolanda herself, he guessed. She might not have gone ahead with her suicidal plan. Or, if she had, it could have been a family member, there to start the arduous task of cleaning out the property. Unless that was something else the company did for the deceased too? They come in, clean up and - just like that - it's one less stress the family has to contend with.

The front door opened. There was a man standing there. He was tall with ginger hair and piercing green eyes which stared through Greg. Confused as to why Greg was standing on his doorstep a little after half eight in the evening, the man asked, 'Can I help you?'

'Yeah. Can I speak to Yolanda, please?' If the man was related, this is the part of the story where he would tell Greg she had passed away. He'd then close the door to continue his grieving in private, leaving Greg to wonder what the fuck had happened to her. But..

'Who?' The man looked at him blankly. 'I think you have the wrong house, mate.'

Greg shook his head. 'No. I was here only the other week.'

The man laughed. 'I don't think you were, mate.'

'Yep. Came back from the pub with her and fucked her in both her living room and kitchen of all places and...' Greg stopped talking. Behind the man he could see that the decor of the house was completely different now. Yolanda had the walls painted in shades of light blues and - yet - now they were magnolia in colour. 'The fuck?' Greg pushed past the man and stepped in the house.

'What the fuck are you playing at? Get out of my house.' The man grabbed Greg by the shoulders and shoved him back out again but not before Greg took a deep breath in. He'd half expected to smell fresh paint but - nothing. The only thing he could smell was something cooking in the kitchen, or something which had been cooked in there recently. The man continued, 'I don't know your game but you need to fuck off while you still can, you hear me?'

Greg didn't argue with him as he stumbled down the drive, thanks to the stranger's hefty shove. He looked confused and went to ask another question (how long had this man been living there) but the words didn't come out. Instead, he heard Chris say again that Yolanda had never existed. With everything starting to spin, Greg hurried away from the house. The man watched a while and then disappeared back into his home, slamming the front door shut in the process.

As Greg drove home, desperate to sink one of the many bottles of whiskey he had stacked high in his kitchen cupboards, his mind continued to race in various directions. With Chris's words going over and over - saying how Yolanda never existed - Greg found it hard to make much sense of any of the thoughts. He knew this wasn't possible (to make someone just disappear from existence) and yet why would people go to the hassle of pretending she didn't exist to him? Surely it would be too complicated for the company to make this happen with actors all playing their role? Or was it literally *just* that? These people were hired to pretend Yolanda had never existed? If someone mentioned her, they simply said they had never heard of her? With enough people saying it - those asking would soon go mad in their confusion or would soon give up asking because they'd be fed up with people lying? Was that how someone could get "erased" from history? But then if that's the case then where is she now? Buried out in some shallow grave somewhere? Cremated? Did she choose not to go ahead with any of this and move away? The more Greg thought about the whole situation, the more his brain got tangled up in his confusion. Now, the bottle of whiskey was calling.

Desperate to get home so he could drink the day - and memories - away, Greg pressed his foot down harder on the accelerator. Having already had a drink in the bar earlier, before the meeting, he didn't give a shit that he was over the limit and knowing he only had x amount of time left before he "ceased to be", he didn't give a shit about the police either. He just wanted to be home. He just wanted to be alone.

8.

TWO DAYS LATER

Nikki Fontana entered the elevator of Greg's apartment block. She pressed the button for the fifth floor. The doors closed noisily, the lift shuddered and took her to the relevant floor. The doors opened. The smell of weed hit her immediately and she was hit with a feeling of guilt.

Greg had moved into the apartment after their relationship had fallen apart. It wasn't in the nicest of areas, but it was what he could comfortably afford without putting himself in more needless debt. To start with, she'd said he could stay in the house but - he was adamant he wanted to go, after she broke off their relationship. Living "as friends" would have caused more problems than he wanted to face, when he already had enough to be contending with.

Nikki told herself that this was *his* choice. She'd given him the option to stay in the house they shared - for however long it would have been necessary for something better to come along. He had refused it. He had chosen this place. She walked down the long corridors, treading the heavily stained carpets in the process, and got to his front door. She hesitated for a moment, unsure as to whether she should have even been here. Her mind was questioning whether this was a good idea? She couldn't help but feel her brain could have questioned this earlier, before she'd left the house but - here she was.

No sense coming this far and not seeing if he was in anyway. She took in a deep breath to steady her nerves and - then - she knocked the door, unsure as to how he was going to react to her being there.

Greg was staring down at the boiling kettle, waiting for the button to "click" signifying the water was boiled. Nikki was sitting on the only stool he had in the kitchen; it was next to the equally small breakfast bar. When he had first seen the breakfast bar, when he came to look at the accommodation, he couldn't do anything but laugh at why someone would put in such a small bar. Only when the estate agent had told him that the old gentleman, who lived there before, hadn't had any family or friends to share breakfast with, did Greg "get it". If it was "just you" then, there really is no need for anything bigger as it was just a waste of space. That was the moment Greg had made his mind up to take the property.

Nikki started to ask, 'How have you…'

Before she finished her sentence, Greg cut her off and told her, 'Please don't.'

'Don't what?'

'You realise that whenever you see me, or talk to me, the first thing you do is ask how I have been?'

'It's called being polite. It's what people do when they talk to their friends. Especially when they haven't seen them for a while. They ask how they have been.'

'If you say so.' Greg thought she only asked him because of his depression and the fact he'd tried taking his own life. Before the last attempt, people had very rarely asked how he was. They would just see him and immediately start talking about their lives as though his didn't matter. Not once did they stop to ask about his day. The moment he tried to take his own life though, it seemed as though - suddenly - everyone gave a shit. The problem was, he knew that - deep down - they didn't. Sure, they asked how he was but really, if he then answered truthfully, they would have run a fucking mile. It also annoyed the shit out of him that it took a couple of suicide attempts to get them asking in the first place. Still, usually, he always answered the same: *I'm fine.* With Nikki though, he couldn't be bothered to play that song and dance. He just wanted the bullshit left at the doorstep although, truth be told, he had no idea why she was sitting in his kitchen waiting for a cup of tea. He thought he had been clear enough with her the last time they spoke, just after his last doctor's appointment.

Greg asked, 'What do you want?'

'I wanted to make sure you were okay.'

'I don't need your pity.'

'You know, you can be a real arsehole sometimes. I'm not here out of pity. I am here because I hadn't heard from you. You've been ignoring my calls and I was worried about you.'

'I've been ignoring your calls because you're with whatever his name is now. I don't want to get in the way of your relationship.'

Nikki laughed.

'What's so funny?'

'There is no relationship. We aren't together anymore.'

'Oh…'

'Had you answered the phone, I might have been able to tell you that, and everything else that I've been doing but - no - you chose to ignore me.'

'I didn't know.'

'Why would you?'

The kettle boiled. Greg grabbed the handle and lifted the kettle from its cradle. Silently he poured her a tea before setting the kettle back down again. Nikki watched as Greg finished making her drink. With a quick stir of a small spoon, he moved her cup over to the breakfast bar where she had made herself comfortable.

'Thank you,' she said.

After a slight pause, Greg couldn't hold his question in anymore and asked, 'What happened?'

'We just weren't a good fit.' There really was nothing else to say about it. Sometimes you just know when a relationship isn't right. If you're adult about it, you can back out before anyone really gets hurt. The best kind of break-up, if a break-up is necessary in the first place. With nothing else to say on the subject, Nikki changed the topic of conversation back to Greg, 'What about you?'

'What about me what?'

'You look like hell. What happened to you?'

Greg forced a smile. He said again, 'I'm fine.' He wasn't fine though. Since finding out about the whole "being wiped from existence", Greg had spent his days locked away in his apartment and drinking heavily. As Yolanda once said to him, *a drunk day is better than a sober day*. He changed the subject again, as though they were taking it turns in just batting it back to one another. 'Why are you really here?' Greg knew Nikki well. They had been a partnership for a couple of years, and, from her face, he could tell there was more to her visit than just to check up on him.

Nikki stumbled over her words a bit as she told him, 'I… I didn't want to be alone.' With that, she started to weep. Greg just stood there a moment. It had been so long since he had been confronted with someone else's emotions, he didn't really know what to do. A second later and he walked over to her; he crouched down and embraced her. It was fair to say the break-up hadn't been quite as "easy" as she had implied.

9.

'I'm sorry about that,' Nikki said as she walked into the living room from the bathroom. They had moved the conversation through to the living room, where it was more comfortable. Nikki had explained that James had been cheating on her with an ex and - when confronted about it - had turned aggressive. Instead of apologising or even trying to defend his actions, he simply shrugged and told Nikki he was only with her because things weren't quite smooth sailing "at home". His plan had supposedly been to move out for a little while whilst they worked things out. A little space to heal the rift, so to speak. Or that other old saying about absence making the heart grow fonder. Nikki didn't know if the other woman even knew about her. She presumed not, given the fact James was moving back in with her. After all, had Nikki been the "other" woman patiently waiting at home for her boyfriend to work shit out with her - she wouldn't have taken it kindly to then find out that he had been fucking around during their break. 'I guess I wasn't as "okay" about it as I thought I was,' Nikki said as she took her seat next to Greg.

'It's okay. Better to let it all out.'

'I guess. I just didn't mean to do it in front of you.'

'Scared it will tip me over the edge?'

Nikki looked at him, disappointed he'd suggest such a thing. She corrected him, 'No - because it's not your problem. I didn't want to bog you down with it.'

'It's always better to talk about your problems.'

Nikki looked at him in total disbelief. She wasn't sure if he was being serious or not. If he was then - how? He had twice tried to take his own life. Had he talked about his problems, that might not have happened. At the very least - had he talked of his problems openly - they probably wouldn't have split up anyway. That was, after all, one of the reasons as to why they had broken apart; because he was so closed off. Greg started to laugh. *Joking.*

'You're an idiot,' she said. With that she playfully slapped his arm. She too laughed though and that was better than crying.

'You know you can always talk to me about things,' Greg said.

Nikki's laughter subsided. She patted him on the arm and told him, 'I can't though, can I?' Just as she had tried to get him to talk before, when they were a couple, she also tried to talk to him too. Whenever she did, he just walked away. Greg knew those past moments were what prompted her response now.

'You ever realise how other people's problems are always easy to solve?' Greg said after a short pause.

'What do you mean?'

'Our own problems feel like mountains. Like mountains we can't climb. We can't even see the top of them. They're up there, hidden in the clouds. But when someone else has a problem, we look at it and it's something small. Simple to fix. We explain to the other person how to get over it. They don't listen though because - how can something so complicated, to them, be fixed so easily? And it goes the other way too. They look at our problems as insignificant too. They have ways to help us. Ways for us to fix it but - again -we don't listen either.' Greg paused a moment and then said, 'If we listened to each other… We could probably live happier lives, but we never seem to be able to trust other people to be able to help us. We listen to their advice but there's always a reason as to why we don't follow it through.' He stopped talking. Nikki was just looking at him. *Where had this attitude been back when it was needed?*

'Shame you learned that lesson too late then, I guess,' Nikki said. She was referring to the lesson being too late to save their relationship, unaware of it being too late to save his life. Greg just smiled at her and looked down to the tattoo on his wrist. Nikki said, 'I still can't believe you got that, Mr. I Don't Like Tattoos.'

'I can't believe it either,' Greg said quietly. 'Guess it's all part of a new me…'

Nikki said, 'So long as you don't change too much from the old you…' She leaned in closer to Greg. He looked at her and their eyes locked. She leaned closer still and then kissed him on the lips before pulling away. 'I'm sorry,' she said.

Greg grabbed her and pulled her closer to him. She didn't resist as he kissed her back with a passion neither of them had felt together for far too long.

10.

Nikki was snoozing in Greg's embrace. The pair of them were in his bed. Their clothes were in crumpled heaps on the floor from where they'd ripped them off one another as they fell into the bedroom, still kissing. The sex had been fast and frantic. It was less about making love and more about "fucking".

Greg wasn't dozing. He was staring up at his discoloured ceiling. Whilst there was a confusion hanging heavy about how this had all just happened, given how distant he thought the pair were, he didn't regret a moment of it. For the briefest of moments, it reminded him of the past, before the depression took a hold. Everything was calm between Nikki and Greg, they'd had plans to travel together when they both turned forty (their birthdays were in the same year, just a few months apart) and the world just seemed "right". It had cruised along like that for a while too, right up until that black cloud descended over Greg, seemingly from out of nowhere. According to forums and groups he was a part of, that was fairly common. One minute everything could be a-okay and the next, you could feel as though your world was crumbling down around you and there would be nothing you could do to change it. It was horrible and for a while he tried to swallow it down but - it wasn't long before cracks in his personality and demeanour started to change and… Well… The rest of the story was obvious.

Greg glanced down to Nikki. She looked so beautiful, even if she had just been fucked two ways from Sunday. He had hated putting her through all he'd done, just as he had hated putting his parents through it too. As his thoughts continued going in the same guilty circles that they'd been going in for so long now, Nikki stirred. She caught him looking at her and smiled in response. He didn't smile, not because he didn't want to but because he was worried about what all of this meant. If she had just wanted to blow off some steam then, great. If she was expecting more from him then, he just couldn't give her any promises anymore. Not just because he knew the black dog of depression still hounded him but because he also knew his life now had a definite timer ticking down. Sure, the latter could be said for everyone but - not everyone knew the date they were going to die.

Nikki asked, 'What you thinking?'

Greg smiled at her and said, 'Nothing. Just switched off. Enjoying the calm.' It was easier than saying what was on his mind. He knew if he said that, it would just trigger an argument. One he couldn't be bothered to have. That was another good thing about knowing your date of death; you didn't spend as much time arguing with people. You just let whatever was wrong slide away and got on with your day. It was just a shame that people who didn't know their "end date" didn't do the same; everyone would be so much happier in their lives.

Nikki cuddled in closer to him before she admitted, 'I've missed you.'

Greg looked back up to the ceiling and just smiled in response. A response that Nikki didn't exactly appreciate. She had hoped to hear the same back from him. She sat up and scooted over to the edge of the bed.

'What's wrong?' Greg asked.

'Nothing,' she lied. Then, she thought better of lying and admitted to him, 'I'm sorry. I shouldn't have come here.'

Greg didn't argue with her, which further rammed her own latest thought home harder. She shook her head and started to pick her clothes up from the floor. Greg watched as she started to put them on. Watching her, he couldn't tell if she was in a mood with him or about to burst into tears. He wanted to say something but didn't know the words to use. Was he meant to apologise for being an arsehole? But then - what had he done other than kiss her back? She was the one who had showed up on his doorstep. She was the one who had kissed him first. He'd just responded as many men would have. Besides, whatever happened between them, he did still love her on whatever level someone like him could "love" on. He just knew it wasn't *enough* for her.

When she was fully dressed she turned to look at him one last time. He hadn't moved from the bed at all and didn't look as though he were about to either. From his body language, he was more than happy to let her walk out of the room and - possibly - his life. A tear rolled down her cheek. It really was over.

Nikki said, 'We had some good times, didn't we?'

Greg smiled at her. 'Yes.'

'I'll cherish them,' she told him. With that, she walked from the bedroom. Greg stayed put as - from out in the hallway - the front door opened and closed.

'Me too,' he whispered.

Greg was standing in front of a mirror in his small bathroom. He was still naked from earlier. The shower was running scolding hot water where he'd turned it on to warm it up, ahead of a shower.

Greg kept thinking about what Nikki had said about cherishing the good memories. His thoughts didn't stop there. He was thinking about all the good memories he had had with her, with friends and with his family. Happy memories long since dimmed with black thoughts and self-hatred. It wasn't so much as a "happy play-back"; he was thinking about the thoughts because, whilst it wouldn't matter to him as he wouldn't be there anymore, he would be robbing those he had once loved of their happier memories. If the company was telling the truth, and they could just make it so someone never even existed, then all positive memories would just disappear. If that were the case - just one of the many burning questions he had was - what would replace those lost memories?

Greg had hated the look in the eyes of those he loved, after he'd attempted to take his life. He could see that they were hurting badly. They blamed themselves, they didn't know how to "fix" him, they worried that he might try it again - all of this was clear in the way they looked at him and, yes, he hated it. But what would be better? To know they lost him to suicide but still have those happy memories to cling to or to never have any knowledge of him whatsoever? He tried to shake the thought from his mind. The whole thing about what Chris Hall had told him was stupid. Greg didn't know how they did it but there was no way on Earth they could just make it as though someone never existed. No way. And Greg could prove it.

11.

Eloisa Velazquez had never spoken much during the weekly sessions with the rest of the group. Chris never pushed her to say anything. They were made to come as part of the agreement they'd made but, they weren't ever forced to talk unless they specifically wanted to. Eloisa seemed happy enough just listening to the others recount how they were spending their last months on the planet.

During the last session she had finally chosen to say something more than her name. It was in the final minutes, just after Chris had said to the group that he would see them the following week, at the same time. Eloisa had simply stood up and said, 'I won't be here next week.' No one said anything. As one of the "oldest" faces of the group, they knew what she meant. For the sake of clarity, she held up her wrist to show the Death's-Head moth tattoo.

Chris asked her, 'How do you feel?'

Eloisa smiled. She said quietly, 'I feel good.'

'No regrets?'

She shook her head. It was natural to wonder what had brought her to this stage of her life and whether she had found a new zest for life in the last year but, no one ever asked. A strange silence fell amongst the group members. No one knew what to say. What was the protocol for this? Wish her a good journey? Hug her goodbye? No one said anything. Quietly the group started to leave as Chris said his individual goodbyes at the door. On the off chance someone wanted to say something, Eloisa waited until near the end. When she got to the door, Chris said to her, 'I'll call you to arrange the transfer of payment.'

Eloisa nodded and - quietly - left the room unaware (as was everyone) that the shadows in the room seemed to be following her. Chris closed the door behind her and turned back to Greg, who was patiently waiting to continue his earlier conversation about Yolanda.

Greg knocked on Eloisa's front door unsure as to whether anyone would answer. From seeing her tattoo at the last meeting, he had managed to work out when her last day was but - that didn't mean he knew *what time* her last hour would be. For all he knew, she was already gone, and a stranger was about to open the door.

The door opened and Greg was relieved to see Eloisa standing there. She was wearing a pink dressing gown. Her make-up had been smudged down her face from where she'd been crying.

Unsure what to say to her, Greg simply said, 'Hi.'

Eloisa was surprised to see Greg. She asked, 'Are you here to do it?' Greg spotted an opportunity to get into her home without being turned away. He nodded. She said, 'I didn't realise you worked for them. I thought you were just another member.' She took a step back and welcomed him in. She closed the door behind him.

The inside of the house was mostly empty. Furniture had been sold, or given away, and there weren't any pictures hanging on the walls. Greg followed Eloisa through to the living room. In the middle of the room there was a shoe box. It was open, with the lid next to it, and seemingly full of old photos Eloisa had kept over the years. When she noticed Greg looking in the box's direction, she simply smiled and said, 'Memories.' She added, 'Thought I would go with happy thoughts, you know?'

Greg nodded. 'Better to go out with a smile,' he said.

'I've waited so long for today. It's weird that it's finally here,' Eloisa said as she made herself comfortable next to the box. She started to go through the pictures once again as Greg stood close by, watching. 'I dug all of these out and put them in the shoe-box so that you could pass them onto my family,' Eloisa said. 'Hopefully - one day - they'll be able to look at them and smile.'

'Hopefully'

'There's some nice pictures in here.'

Greg didn't have the heart to tell her what Chris had told him; that she would simply cease to exist, along with all trace of her - meaning the photos would vanish too.

Eloisa continued, 'Looking back through them, it makes me wonder if I am making a mistake. Maybe I should take the pills again and try them? Maybe this time they'll work? Or counselling? I might get a better therapist?'

Greg said nothing.

Eloisa looked directly at him and said, 'Sorry - what did you say?'

'I didn't say anything.' Greg wasn't there for conversation. He was there to see what would happen to Eloisa. So long as she didn't change her mind, Greg was expecting one of Chris's colleagues to come in any moment now and put her down, just as they had promised. Then he would see that the group members didn't just "disappear" but, instead, how it was a carefully crafted mission to clean away any trace of them. No magic disappearing act, just team-work and people happy to deny someone's existence. *That was it.*

'I didn't say I had changed my mind,' Eloisa said.

'I didn't say you did.'

'You did. I just heard you.' She explained, 'I was just saying - what if this is a mistake? What if I *could* turn things around for myself and find a way to live happily? I'm not sure how given I have tried everything offered but...' She held up the photos and asked, 'What if I can make more memories like this?'

'Only you would know that,' Greg said.

Eloisa snapped, 'I'm not changing my mind...'

'I never said anything.' The more Greg watched her, the stranger her behaviour appeared to be. But then, how was she supposed to act? For all he knew, he would be like this too - when his time came. He went on to say, 'Look even if you are changing your mind, there is nothing wrong with that.'

Eloisa shouted at him, 'You just said I couldn't change my mind!'

'I didn't...'

Then, inexplicably, the room seemed to get darker despite it still being bright outside.

'If you're going to do it, just do it!' Eloisa snapped at Greg. He didn't respond. He just stood there, confused as to what was happening. He had noticed the brightness in the room dim right down but, she clearly hadn't. After less than a couple of seconds, Eloisa shouted, 'Fine! I'll do it myself!' She turned and walked from the room as Greg continued to just stand there, watching dumbfounded. He noticed the dimness of the room seemed to follow her. When she left the room, everything went back to its original brightness. He went after her. When he reached the hallway, the bathroom door at the far end of it slammed shut. From behind the door, Eloisa screamed. Greg hurried down the hallway and yanked open the door only to find the room was empty. With no clear way out, she had literally just vanished into nothing.

'Eloisa?'

There was no answer. With Chris's words echoing in his mind, he stepped back out of the bathroom and into the hallway. Immediately he noticed that the colour of the walls was different than a second ago. So too were the carpets different.

'The fuck?'

Greg looked up the hallway and froze. At the far end, close to the kitchen door, there was a small black child standing there with a packet of crisps in his hands and a shocked look on his face. For a moment, neither of them spoke until, suddenly, the young child screamed, 'Dad! There's someone in our house!'

The suddenness of the child's shout pulled Greg right back into the moment. He didn't wait to see who this child's father was. He turned and ran for the front door which was, mercifully, close by.

The drive home was a heady mixture of panic and questions. What had happened to Eloisa? He could still hear her scream as though it were happening right now. He'd never heard such a cry before, at least not from a human. A scream full of fear and - more noticeably - pain. *What had happened to her*? How had she just been pulled from existence and how the hell did her place just change like that? One minute she was there and the next she was gone, and another family was living there. How does that even happen? Another part of his brain was worrying about his friends, family and even Nikki. What happened to Yolanda and Eloisa would also be happening to him soon enough and - when that time came - all their good memories, the ones they'd want to hold onto, would be taken away from them. That very thought twisted his stomach more than anything. It was one thing to end his own life but to take things away from their lives?   Especially things that they would want... He hadn't signed up for that.

12.

'But you did though,' Chris said.

Chris was on the other end of the phone. Greg had phoned his "emergency contact number" the moment he'd got back to his shitty little apartment.

Chris continued, 'At the end of the year you want us to take your life, yes? You want us to make it so your family are "okay", yes? Take a look at Eloisa. She is gone from this world, just as she wanted. Those close to her are none the wiser about what happened. They have no pain; they have no regrets or guilt or anything. They are simply living a life in blissful ignorance.'

'But you've taken all of their happy memories. What do those get replaced by? Or do those left behind just have black spots?'

'They have memories of a life they'd have had as if she had never existed. Same with those close to Yolanda and - when the time comes - those close to you. Take your parents for example: They might have had a different child. So, they'll have happy memories of this other kid. As I said, they'll have no guilt or upset about the son they had who killed himself. You'll be gone from this world, those close to you - when you were here - will be happy in whatever life they've had without you. The end result is exactly what we promised.'

'And what if the other memories aren't as nice for them?'

'What if this? What if that? You can play this game all day long, but nothing changes. You signed up for this and this is the way everything works.'

'No. I'm backing out. I'm done. I'm not a part of this. I didn't agree to having you wipe their memories of me. This is just…' Greg stopped. He didn't know what this was. Was he being selfish in making them keep the memories? Could they have better memories without him in the world? His head continued to spin; its permanent state since finding Yolanda had been pulled from reality.

Chris sighed. 'You can't pull out. We have an agreement, and you have the mark.'

'The tattoo? So what? It's a fucking tattoo.' Greg said defiantly, 'Then I won't pay you the money.'

Chris laughed. 'It's not about the money. Think about it. What happens to you at the end of all of this? You disappear. You never existed. Because you never existed, we technically never had the deal and you never paid me the money. You realise, when you disappear so does everything you have ever done and owned. And - sadly - that includes the money.'

'Then if you're not getting the money you can just stop all this.'

'It's not down to me, I'm afraid. It's Him. I have the deal with him. All I have to do is feed him people such as yourselves and in exchange, I get rewarded with something more than money can buy.'

'Him? Who the fuck is "Him"?'

Chris laughed. 'Who do you think? Death. The Grim Reaper. You do realise suicides go to purgatory right? There's no Heaven or Hell for them. Purgatory. It's those souls which are left behind that he gets to feast upon and - let me tell you - Death is hungry.'

Greg wanted to shout and scream down the phone. He wanted to tell Chris he was crazy. He wanted to scream how he was full of shit but, the problem was, he knew he wasn't. Not now he had seen it for himself.

Chris continued, 'Those who carry His mark are destined to be consumed by him. That's how it works, and I am sorry but there is no way back for you. Not now.'

Silence fell between them.

With such a quiet line, Chris was forced to ask, 'Are you still there?'

'Why are you doing this?'

'Do you know how long I have been doing this? Ninety years, give or take.' To look at, Chris didn't look a day over forty at most. 'Don't look my age, do I? I was like you once. I went to take my own life, but it didn't go to plan. Death visited me and that's where he offered me the deal. I can feed him people like you, and he can keep giving me time on this planet.'

'You tried to kill yourself and chose to live forever?'

Chris laughed. 'Death said he would come back to me in a year. He told me to live that year and be sure it was what I really wanted - to die, that is. If it was, he would take me as requested but also offer me something else. It was the last part of his sentence that got my interest. I wanted to know what else he could offer. So, I went and lived my life and - as I explained to you when you signed up - things changed for me. The depression went away because I knew the day I was going to die. Anyway, when Death came back he offered to take me or leave me here to work for him. I just had to feed him souls like you.'

'Lots of people kill themselves every day. Surely he has enough to eat.'

'Doesn't taste as good as those who have changed their mind.'

'What?'

'In the last year, do you know how many people come to me and tell me they aren't ready to die yet? They ask for more time - if only one more year. When Death comes for them, he comes when they don't *want* to die. They still count as a suicide though because it was their choice and so he still gets to feast upon them, but they taste better. More nutritious for him. There's no Heaven or Hell for them, like I said. There's just Death and his insatiable hunger.'

'But if they're changing their mind... That becomes murder.'

'It's a grey area, I'll give you that but - when they signed up - they had their choice to back away. Each and every person wanted to die when they signed up. They knew what they were getting into.'

'But we didn't though! We didn't know this!'

'Are you honestly saying that - if you had, and you had believed it - you would have not signed up? Mr. I'm-so-suicidal? What does it matter how you die? What does it matter if your loved ones don't remember you? You didn't want to be here. I'm doing people like you a favour. What, now you know mummy and daddy won't have those happy memories to hold onto, you want to quit out? Pretty selfish, Greg.'

'Fuck you. I want out!'

'Sorry, no can do. You have his mark. We can have this conversation right up until He comes to get you but, honestly, I can't help but feel this is a waste of your time so...' Chris disconnected the call.

Greg screamed out in frustration and launched his mobile across the room. It shattered against the wall and fell to the floor. He dropped to his knees. He didn't cry, he didn't scream. He just froze up as the whole conversation slowly sunk in. None of it sounded real. Instead, everything came across as nothing more than some kind of nightmare. But no matter how many times he pinched himself, he knew he wouldn't wake up. Worse yet, he knew no one would believe him if he told them about it. But who would he tell? Greg had burned most bridges of his friendships long ago. Instead of letting his friends be there for him, in his hour of need, he simply pushed them away because it was "easier". He could tell the group about what Chris had said but -

again - would they even give a shit, even if they believed him? Kneeling there, in his cold and empty apartment, he knew he was more alone than he had ever been. As Greg screamed out in frustration for a second time, his neighbour banged on the wall and yelled for him to shut the hell up. Greg immediately jumped up and slammed himself against the wall with the whole of his body.

'You shut the fuck up, you piece of shit!' Greg started pounding on the wall over and over. A thought flashed to mind that if he was going to suddenly disappear from existence, and all he'd done would be wiped from history, there was nothing stopping him from going around and stamping his irritating neighbour to death. But then, why stop there? Why not find all those who had wronged him and hurt them too? Enjoy the last months wreaking as much havoc as he possibly could. Start with his neighbour and then find James Steel, the prick who'd hurt Nikki. It would have been an absolute pleasure to find him and run a knife across his scrawny little throat. Maybe even film it so Nikki could get some satisfaction from it too... *What*? Nikki hated violence so why did he think it would be a good idea to show her what he had done? *Get a grip of yourself.*

A few more fist-slams into the wall and he slumped down it, exhausted. He half expected his neighbour to come round and get in his face, or - at the very least - hit the wall back but, there was silence. For his neighbour's benefit, it was probably just as well given Greg's dark mood. It wouldn't have taken that much more to encourage him to go around and kick his head in.

13.

Greg's alarm was ringing by the side of his bed. 6:00am. It hadn't needed to ring in order to wake him up as he'd not slept all night. Instead, he had simply tossed and turned, unable to shut off his brain for just a minute. In his mind's eye he just kept seeing Chris's smug face staring back at him. He kept hearing what he had told him, both face to face and over the phone. Not just that though - he kept seeing Nikki's face. That crushed look in her eyes when he hadn't admitted to missing her right back, after she had told him the same. And her voice: Telling him how she would cherish the good times they'd had together even if it was over between them. On top of all of that though - there was the thought of Death itself. This figure he had always presumed to have been the figment of someone's imagination, much like how Jesus was to him. Someone came up with the idea of a religious man, they told a friend, the idea took off and - before you knew it - it spread through the world. Greg never actually thought there was a real Grim Reaper stalking the shadows, collecting those who had perished. There was a small part of him which still thought it bullshit too but that didn't help his brain shut off, thinking it all a lie. If it was bullshit, then how had that house changed appearance before his very eyes?

On the rare occasions Greg had drifted off, his dreams were not kind. As if haunted by Eloisa's last scream, he dreamed of coming face to face with Death himself. What He must have looked like to get such a reaction from Eloisa. In old films, and vivid descriptions written in literature, Death is pictured as a menacing, cloaked skeletal being with a scythe. Was that who had confronted Eloisa? Was her final sight, this unearthly monster swinging his scythe down upon her, thereby erasing her from history? That was what Greg had seen in his nightmares. He had been standing there, surrounded by darkness, when - suddenly - Death appeared before him with His skeletal smile and eyes so blue fixed upon Greg. Without a word, He raised His scythe and swung down hard, splitting Greg clean in two. Any other night, it would have been a foolish nightmare to have. So stupid and so unrealistic in its nature that it wouldn't have caused so much as a quickened heartbeat in Greg's chest but - with what he knew - now the thought was terrifying.

'Fuck you! I want out.'

'Sorry, no can do. You have his mark,' the words played through Greg's mind along with the nightmarish images of Death and Eloisa's scream until - another thought popped to mind. Tattoo's weren't as permanent as they once had been.

Greg winced in discomfort as the tattooist, Andrew Southern, worked the laser; the equipment needed to remove the ink from Greg's wrist. They'd gone through all of the necessary information about what it would take to remove the tattoo and the healing process. The fact there'd be pain for about a week and the site would potentially blister up. Greg hadn't paid any attention. He didn't care about the pros and cons of going through with all of this. He just wanted the tattoo gone.

'It's a shame,' Andrew said.

'What is?'

'It's a nice tattoo. Whoever did it, they did a good job.'

'Yeah.'

As Andrew continued working the area, he asked, 'So what's the story? How come you want to get rid of it? Remind you of an ex, or something?'

'Something like that.'

Andrew pulled a face as though to say, *Excuse me for asking*. He continued working in silence. Greg didn't want to get into the reason he had the tattoo, or the reason he wanted it gone. There was zero point. He knew Andrew would just think he was taking the piss.

Andrew changed the subject and asked, 'How's the pain?'

Greg smiled. He didn't mind the pain. It reminded him of the days he used to self-harm; the days where he had actually *felt* something. 'It's fine,' Greg said.

'That's good. Some people find it really uncomfortable.'

'Well, I'm good.'

'If you need to take a break, just say.'

'I said I'm good.'

'Okay, just saying…'

Greg turned away from watching what was going on. He looked over to the wall and the posters stuck up there. He hoped that, if he looked like he was reading, Andrew would just shut up and get on with his job. It didn't work.

'Might need a couple of runs at this to really get it done,' the tattooist said.

'What?'

'Happens sometimes. Depends how they've been done but, yeah, sometimes it can take a couple of goes to remove it completely.'

'No. I want it all gone now.'

'Well obviously I'm going to try my best but, just warning you again. I mean, I did tell you before we started.'

'It needs to be gone today.'

Andrew laughed. 'Well technically you won't see it when you leave. I'll be wrapping it in a bandage.'

Greg didn't find this funny. He came to the appointment to get the tattoo removed, not *half-removed*. Greg told him, 'So if you only get rid of half of the tattoo then I only pay for a half a job, right?'

Again, the tattooist laughed. 'Yeah, it doesn't work like that. Paying for my time.'

Greg didn't have a comeback for that. He glanced back down to his wrist and watched as the tattooist continued working at the artwork stained there. *Please let it all go today. Please.* Chris had said that he couldn't back out of the deal because he had the mark on him. Without the mark, surely there would be no deal. *Surely*?

'You still good?' Andrew glanced up to Greg's face. Usually people were squirming a lot more than Greg was.

Greg said, 'Just keep going…'

'You're the boss.'

Greg put his head back and closed his eyes. It seemed the more Andrew brought up the possibility of "pain", the more the procedure started to hurt. Now, he just wanted it done.

By the time Greg got back into his car, his wrist was throbbing with pain. He hadn't seen the end result of what the tattooist had managed to do, before his wrist had been wrapped. He hadn't even closed his car door before he started pulling at the bandage so he could see if it was gone.

'What the fuck?' He stared at his bare skin in dismay. There was no sore patch, there was no blistering, there was nothing but a perfect tattoo of a Death's Head Moth. Weirder still was how it didn't even look a few months old anymore. It looked fresh and vibrant. It looked perfect. Greg asked again, 'What the fuck is this?' He looked around in a hope there'd be someone close to his car. Someone he could ask, *Can you see this tattoo*? Maybe they wouldn't be able to see it? Maybe only he could because it was part of the deal he had made? In reality - his wrist could look sore from having it removed but, other than that, normal? No one was in the immediate vicinity of where he was sitting but - he could see Andrew standing out the front of his tattoo shop, a cigarette in his hand.

Greg jumped out of his car, slammed the door and hurried over to the tattooist. He shouted, 'Is this a fucking joke?'

Andrew looked at him as though Greg had lost his mind.

'Look!' Greg held his wrist up. Andrew didn't need him to explain what the problem was as he saw the tattoo with his own eyes.

'What the hell?' Andrew grabbed Greg's hand when he was close enough and brought it up closer to his face so he could get a clearer look at the tattoo. He started to laugh.

'What's so funny?! I paid you to remove the fucking thing!'

'You watched me! I did!' Andrew explained, 'I'm laughing because I thought it was a dream...'

'What the fuck are you talking about?'

'When I saw your tattoo, I remembered what I thought was a dream. Some person - I can't recall who, not even whether it was a man or a woman - came into my shop asking me to remove the very same tattoo. I did the job and a couple days later they came back saying it had come back.' He explained, 'When I remembered it all, I just thought it was a weird dream I had after a night on the whiskey but... Well either it was a premonition to you coming in or there's some of you guys fucking with me.' He looked around. 'Is there a hidden camera somewhere? You have an identical twin, and they came in earlier to remove the tattoo? Is that how it works?' He laughed again. 'Sorry, mate, not falling for it...'

Greg stood for a moment with one over-riding thought racing through his mind; he wanted to punch the prick straight in the face. Before he acted on impulse, he hurried back to his car. He jumped in and wasted no time in driving away from the tattoo shop. In his rear-view mirror he could still make out the tattooist laughing his arse off.

Greg wasn't laughing. He glanced back to the tattoo. If anything, it looked darker now than it had when it was first done. He pulled up behind a car at a red traffic stop and started punching the steering wheel as he screamed over and over, 'Fuck, fuck, fuck, fuck....'

14.

'Did you find your friend?' The barman put Greg's fifth pint down in front of where he was perched at the bar without questioning why Greg was getting so drunk at such an "early" time of the day. The time was a little after two in the afternoon. Sure, enough people liked to drink "more" at this time during the weekends but not normally in the middle of the week and - today was Wednesday.

The barman's name was Keith Crawford. He had worked in the quaint little pub for a little over three years now. The wages were crap but the perks good. As well as being the manager of the bar, he was given access to the apartment in the upper-story of the building. It was the little apartment which made the job worth sticking with. Especially when you took into consideration the amount of rent people usually paid to live in the centre of town.

Greg was staring at his tattoo, lost in deep thought about his predicament. He wasn't thinking about Yolanda and - as a result - had no idea what Keith was talking about. He looked up at him. The bar around him didn't look as crisp in his vision as it had when he first arrived. Now everything seemed a little blurry to him but that didn't bother Greg for he knew it meant the alcohol was doing what it was supposed to: numbing everything. 'What are you talking about?' he asked Keith.

'Your friend? The one you were looking for not so long ago? Sorry, I don't remember their name. Just wondered if you managed to catch up with them?'

Greg realised who he was talking about and bluntly replied, 'They're dead.'

'Shit.' Keith didn't know what to say. He was just standing there with a stupid look on his face until he eventually said, 'Sorry.'

'Want to see a magic trick?' Greg said out of the blue.

'What?' Keith heard what his drunk customer said, he just didn't understand where the question had come from. Not many people were able to go from saying their friend was dead to asking about a magic trick.

Greg asked again, 'Do you want to see a magic trick?'

Regardless of how weird the jump in conversation had been - it was still a good way out of the hole Keith had dug about the deceased friend. He said, 'Sure.'

'I'll need that,' Greg said as he pointed over to a knife at the far end of the bar. For some of his time there, Greg had been watching the barman slice up some lemons ahead of what he must have presumed to be a busy shift.

'The knife?' Instantly Keith was a little more wary. You didn't need to be a genius to know that drunks and knives didn't tend to be a good mix. 'What's it for?'

Greg smiled. 'I already told you. It's for a magic trick.'

Keith hesitated a moment. He weighed up his options in his mind: Give a drunk person a knife and hope he didn't accidentally hurt himself or deny the drunk person his request and potentially have him kick off. It was easier to see what he had planned. Anyway, it wasn't the biggest of blades and if he tried anything stupid with it, Keith could have just snatched it back. He walked across the other side of the bar and took the knife. When got back to where Greg was perched, he handed it over - with the handle pointing towards Greg. At least that way CCTV wouldn't be showing him to be stabbing Greg if he suddenly lunged himself against it, not that Keith thought he would be doing that.

Keith said, 'So come on then, what's this trick?'

'Watch.'

Without further word or explanation, Greg rolled his sleeve up before he turned the knife inwards.

'Hang on, what are you…' Before the barman's words escaped his mouth, Greg stabbed down repeatedly into his own wrist. He penetrated the skin where his tattoo was with such force and ferocity that - within seconds - the tattoo was barely recognisable. 'What the fuck are you doing!' Keith leaned forward and grabbed both Greg's wrist and hand. There was a short struggle before he wrestled the knife away from him. Greg just sat there and laughed as blood ran from his wrist, down onto the bar and floor. 'Get the fuck out of here,' Keith yelled.

'Wait… You haven't seen the magic trick.'

'Just get the fuck out of here before I call the police, you crazy fuck. And don't bother coming back either.'

'You need to see this. Just wait. I promise you it will be worth it.'

Keith walked around from the back of the bar. 'I said get the fuck out of here.' He grabbed Greg by his good arm and walked him from the establishment as others watched on, shocked at what they'd seen. Greg was still laughing as he was shoved from the building. When the door slammed shut behind him, he looked down to his wrist and - lo and behold - the wounds were gone. The tattoo was there.

Greg shouted through the door, 'It's fucking magic!' But it wasn't. To him, it was more of a curse now. With everything that had happened, he realised he wasn't ready to die yet. At least - not like this. Not to be wiped from existence and a snack to some other world being. Still talking about his "magic trick", he said, 'Whatever I do to it, it'll just keep coming back to exactly the same spot... *Whatever I...*' He froze a moment as a thought raced through his mind. Whatever he did to that spot, the tattoo kept coming back but - his thought - what if the spot wasn't there anymore?

15.

Chris Combs turned the television up in his weed-stinking apartment until the volume bar was maxed out but still, he could hear the screaming from next door. He thought it wouldn't be as bad when the buzzing stopped but - it turned out the screaming was just as irritating without the need for the buzz sound too.

'Fuck this,' he said. Out of frustration, he kicked the coffee table in front of him. His mug of tea toppled and spilled the contents down on both table and rug beneath it. In the hope his neighbour could hear him as much as he could hear *him*, Chris screamed, 'Shut the fuck up, you cunt!' His words were either not heard or they were ignored as - through the thin walls - the screaming continued. With his temper boiling over, Chris got up from his stained armchair and left his small apartment. He walked a few steps down the corridor until he was standing at Greg's own front door. He raised his hand and hit the wooden panel with his knuckles. Such was the force of his hit - so he could be sure to be heard - he even marked his knuckles red. 'Open the fucking door!'

Meanwhile other neighbours had come to see what the noise was about too. They didn't approach Greg's door in the same way Chris had though. They were standing in their own doorways, waiting to see how this played out.

After a short delay, Chris kicked the door - not so as to go through it but to be heard and answered. He screamed again, 'I said open the fucking door!'

There was movement from inside the apartment. The buzzing from earlier once again started back up again.

'What the fuck is that fucking noise?!' Chris kicked at the door again but - this time - it swung open and he saw Greg standing there holding a chainsaw in one hand. His other hand was missing from the elbow down. 'What the hell?'

Greg stopped screaming long enough to laugh maniacally. Then he charged forward, and one-handedly swung the spinning blade of the saw towards Chris before Chris himself could react. The saw's teeth chomped into his side and started chewing it up messily. He shrieked in both pain and terror as he pulled himself away from the hungry blade. The neighbours also screamed out. Some just stood there, shocked. Others disappeared back into their apartments, slamming doors shut in the process. One elderly man ran for the elevator down the hall to get away.

Chris slumped down on the floor as blood spilled from his side in such a quantity that it was plain he wouldn't be living for much longer. Had Greg had two hands, he would have already been dead. With the help - and force - of the second hand, Greg could have pushed the blade on through Chris's mid-rift - slicing him clean in two.

Greg dropped the blood-splattered chainsaw to the floor and held up his bloody stump towards the running neighbour. He shouted after him, 'It came back! Look! It came back!' True enough, the tattoo *had* come back. It wasn't in the same spot though, given the wrist was laying on the tiled floor of Greg's kitchen. The tattoo had appeared just above where Greg had amputated his arm and he knew, in that moment, there was no escaping the mark or the fate he had chosen for himself.

Greg fell to his knees and screamed out again. The screaming from within the apartment had been from both pain of cutting away his own lower-arm and also from resentment to his situation. Mostly the pain, which was still very much present. After a few more screams, he glanced down to Chris. He had stopped moving. The pool of blood beneath his body had seeped into the already dirty carpet. Greg didn't feel guilty about the man's death. He'd been a fucking pain in the arse since Greg had moved in but - with the bigger picture - he knew he wasn't really dead. One day Greg would just disappear. All memories of him would be gone. Everything he had done would then be undone. None of what had happened now would come to pass and this little asshole would carry on with his shitty life in blissful ignorance. Greg couldn't help but wonder how that was fair. This drug-selling piece of shit would get to carry on being the cunt that he was, and Greg would be the one sucked from existence. In an ideal world it would be the other way around as Greg wasn't the bad guy. He hadn't gone out of his way to hurt anyone. His only "crime" was to suffer from depression and make stupid mistakes. Other than that, he was harmless.

In the distance he could hear sirens blasting through the air. The police were coming but that wasn't unexpected. No matter where you lived in the world, you couldn't just take a chainsaw to someone - in front of witnesses - and not have the police show up. One of the neighbours must have called them from the perceived safety of their apartment. Greg smiled. Foolish of them, really, to think they were safe in their apartment given he had a chainsaw. If he wanted to get in and attack them, a wooden door wouldn't really stand between them and...

Greg paused.

A thought ran through his mind.

The police were coming. They were answering a call about a deadly attack by an armed man which meant, they wouldn't be coming with truncheons and tasers. They would be coming armed to both defend themselves and properly neutralise the attacker.

Greg stood up. He was unsteady on his feet from the blood loss he'd suffered before he had successfully applied the tourniquet to himself. He put his foot down on the body of the chainsaw, to keep it in place, and then worked the drawstring again to bring the chattering blade back to life. The sirens grew closer still.

The blade buzzed alive once more and Greg picked it up with his one hand. He looked down at Chris's body and smirked. The asshole wouldn't be coming back to life this time and whilst the memory of this very moment might hurt his own family at least - if the plan worked - they would still have the good memories to hold onto as well.

There was a commotion from the stairwell.

The elevators pinged open from the other end of the corridor.

The fire-escape doors opened behind Greg.

The armed response unit of the police burst in with their weapons primed. They started shouting at Greg to put the chainsaw down, warning that - if necessary - they would open fire.

He hoped that they would. If they pulled the trigger, it wouldn't be him taking his own life. Death wouldn't be able to consume his soul. He wouldn't be stuck in purgatory. He would be going to Heaven or - more likely - Hell.

'Put it down!' another officer warned.

Greg smiled and said, 'He was wrong. There is a way out of the deal.' With that, he ran towards the officers over by the elevator. He managed three steps.

AND SO...

Greg's parents had a baby daughter. Her name was Stephanie and she was the apple of their eye. She studied hard and became a doctor, working in a hospital close to where her parents lived.

Nikki married her high-school sweetheart. They stayed together for another fourteen more years before she met another man and parted ways from her former flame. She had two children and three dogs.

Chris Combs continued selling weed to those who'd come by his apartment. He would eventually pass away from cancer at the age of seventy-three.

The "Suicide Club" continues to meet every Friday, sharing stories of how they will be spending their final months, weeks and days.

None of them ever knew Greg.

Chris Hall smiled to himself as he set Greg's file back in the filing closet of his private office. The filing closet was the only proof that any of these people ever existed and would be forever locked - and unseen - to strangers.

As Chris sat down at his desk, the few grey hairs that he had disappeared from both his beard and head. The more he thought about Greg, the more he chuckled. Greg hadn't been the first person to commit suicide by cop and he sure as fuck wouldn't be the last.

There was no way to renege on the deal - not now, not ever.

Enjoyed the stories? Check out Vimeo for some of Matt Shaw's short films!

https://vimeo.com/themattshaw

Want more Matt Shaw?

Sign up for his Patreon Page!

www.patreon.com/themattshaw

Signed goodies?

Head for his store!

www.mattshawpublications.co.uk

CPSIA information can be obtained
at www.ICGtesting.com
Printed in the USA
LVHW090734130621
690102LV00003B/597